Every day Tom Tipper brought th
parcels to the station in his red postvan.
He was always cheerful and he talked to Percy
as he helped to load the mailbags onto the train.

But one day Tom didn't come. A new postman arrived.
He didn't have a red van, he was riding a bicycle.
He dumped the mailbags onto the platform and
rode away without helping.

4

When Tom came back he didn't have a van either, only a bicycle, and he wasn't cheerful any more.

One morning, as Tom arrived, he was called to the stationmaster's office.

He asked Percy to look after his bike
while he was away. But some boys found it
and wheeled it up and down the platform.

The bike went too fast and it roll.... ....m the boys, down the slope and straight into Percy as he was leaving the station. Percy braked hard, but not in time to save the bike.

8

"Sorry, Mr Tipper," said Percy.
"Don't worry. It wasn't your fault, Percy," said Tom.
"I never liked that bike much anyway."

The driver and the guard told the boys
what bad boys they were.
The Fat Controller ordered that Tom
should have a new bike.

But Tom didn't need it.
He was given a shiny new van.

Published by Kaye & Ward,
an imprint of William Heinemann Ltd
Michelin House, 81 Fulham Road
London SW3 6RB
copyright © 1988 William Heinemann Ltd

ISBN 0 434 92742 2
Printed in Hong Kong by Mandarin Offset